Time for Bed, Sleepyheads

By NORMAND and SANDRA CHARTIER

A GOLDEN BOOK, NEW YORK

Western Publishing Company, Inc., Racine, Wisconsin 53404

It is the end of a busy day. Mommies and daddies all over the neighborhood call their children in from play.

"Time for bed, sleepyheads," says Father Raccoon. The kits slowly pick up their toys.

In her home down by the pond, Mother Duck draws a warm bubbly bath. She helps her drowsy ducklings undress and hang up their clothes.

The little ducks splash and soap and scrub—till Mother Duck says, "Out of the tub, now. It's time for bed."

Over in the meadow in a neat little burrow,
Mommy Rabbit dries and powders her sleepy
bunnies. When they are all in clean pajamas,
Mommy gives each baby a squeeze.

"M-m-m-m," she says, "you smell so sweet."

"Don't spill your cocoa," says Papa Possum to his tired little possum. While they share a bedtime snack, they talk about their day.

"Time for bed, sleepyhead," says Mamma.

Small Possum sighs and sips the last drop of cocoa from his cup.

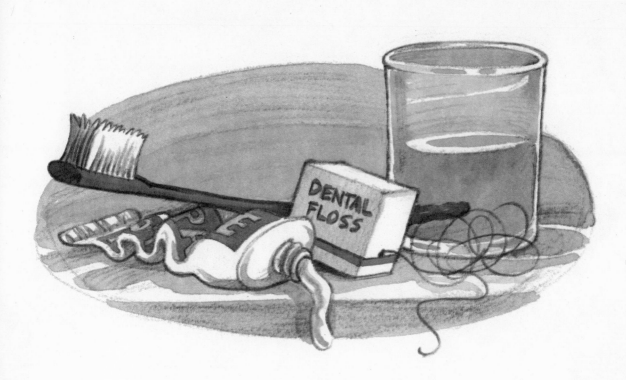

The little beavers busily brush their teeth and rinse their brushes. Daddy Beaver peeks in to make sure their teeth are shining clean.

"Who wants a bedtime story?" he asks.

"We do!" cry two happy little beavers.

The owlets love bedtime stories, too.
"Once upon a time..." begins Mother Owl.
But by the time she reads, "...and they all lived
happily ever after," the little ones' eyelids are
very droopy.

In the Bear Family's cozy den, Mamma Bear
leads her cubs in their bedtime prayers.
  Then the little bears give their mother lots of
good-night hugs and kisses and shuffle off to bed.

"It's time for bed, you sleepyheads," says Mother Goose.

The goslings fluff up their pillows and snuggle down between the sheets. Daddy pulls up the covers and tucks the tired goslings in.

"Lullaby, and good-night!" sings Father Rooster.
His sweet song lulls the chicks to sleep.
Mother Hen turns on the night light.
"Sweet dreams," she whispers as she and Father
tiptoe out and softly shut the door.

Now all is quiet. Stars twinkle in the night sky.
Moonlight shines on every housetop. Sleepyheads
all over the neighborhood are snug in their beds
at last.

Sh-h-h-h-h-h.